To My Father
Virgil

TOM SAWYER

By Mark Twain

Illustrated by
Toby Bluth

Ideals Publishing Corp.
Nashville, Tennessee
ISBN 0-8249-8097-2

"Tom!"
"Tom!"
No answer.
"What's gone with that boy! TOM!"
No answer.

The old lady pulled her spectacles down and looked over them about the room. Then she put them up and looked out under them. She seldom or never looked *through* them for so small a thing as a boy. They were her state pair, the pride of her heart, and were built for "style," not service. She could have seen through a pair of stove lids just as well. She looked perplexed for a moment, and then said, not fiercely, but still loud enough for the furniture to hear,

"Well, if I get hold of you I'll..."

She did not finish, for by this time she was bending down and punching under the bed with the broom, and so she needed breath to punctuate the punches with. She resurrected nothing but the cat.

There was a slight noise behind her and she turned just in time to seize a small boy and arrest his flight.

"There! I might 'a' thought of that closet. What you been doing in there?"

"Nothing."

"Nothing! Look at your
hands. And look at your
mouth. What *is* that?"
   "I don't know, Aunt Polly."
   "Well, *I* know. It's jam—
that's what it is. Forty times I've

said if you didn't let that jam alone I'd skin you. Hand me that switch."

The switch hovered in the air — the peril was desperate.

"My! Look behind you, Aunt Polly!" Tom cried.

The old lady whirled around, and snatched her skirts out of danger. The lad fled on the instant, scrambled up the high board fence, and disappeared over it.

His Aunt Polly stood surprised a moment and then broke into a gentle laugh.

"Hang the boy, can't I never learn anything? Ain't he played me tricks enough like that for me to be looking out for him by this time? But old fools is the biggest fools there is.

"I ain't doing my duty by that boy, and that's the Lord's truth. Spare the rod and spoil the child, as the Good Book says.

"I'll be obliged to make him work tomorrow, to punish him. It's mighty hard to make him work on Saturdays. But he hates work more than he hates anything else, and I've *got* to do some of my duty by him, or I'll be the ruination of the child."

As for Tom, within two minutes, or even less, he had forgotten all his troubles. Not because his troubles were one whit less heavy and bitter to him than a man's are to a man, but because a new and powerful interest bore them down and drove them out of his mind.

This new interest was whistling, which he had just acquired.

Diligence and attention soon gave him the knack of it, and he strode down the street with his mouth full of harmony and his soul full of gratitude.

Presently Tom checked his whistle. A stranger was before him — a boy a shade larger than himself.

This boy was well-dressed — well-dressed on a weekday. This was simply astounding. His cap was a dainty thing, his close-buttoned blue cloth jacket was new and natty, and so were his pants. He had shoes on — and it was only Friday. He even wore a necktie, a bright bit of ribbon.

The more Tom stared at the splendid
marvel, the higher he turned up his nose
at his finery and the shabbier and
shabbier his own outfit seemed to him to
grow. Neither boy spoke. If one moved,
the other moved — but only sideways, in a
circle. They kept face to face and eye to
eye all the time.

Finally Tom said,
"I can lick you!"
"I'd like to see you try it."
"Well, I can do it."
"No you can't either."
"Yes I can."
"No you can't."
"I can!"
"You can't!"

In an instant both boys were rolling and tumbling in the dirt, gripped together like cats; and for the space of a minute they tugged and tore at each other's hair and clothes, punched and scratched each other's noses, and covered themselves with dust and glory. Presently the confusion took form and through the fog of battle Tom appeared, seated astride the new boy and pounding him with his fists.

"Holler 'nuff!" said he.

The boy only struggled to free himself. He was crying,—mainly from rage.

"Holler 'nuff!"—and the pounding went on.

At last the stranger got out a smothered
"Nuff!" and Tom let him up and said,
"Now that'll learn you. Better look out
who you're fooling with next time."

The new boy went off brushing the dust from his clothes, sobbing, snuffling, and occasionally looking back and shaking his head and threatening what he would do to Tom the next time.

Tom got home pretty late that night, and when he climbed cautiously in at the window, he uncovered an ambush, in the person of his aunt; and when she saw the state his clothes were in her resolution to turn his Saturday holiday into captivity at hard labor became unyielding in its firmness.

Saturday morning was come, and all the summer world was bright and fresh and brimming with life.

There was a song in every heart; and if the heart was young the music issued at the lips. There was cheer in every face and a spring in every step. The locust trees were in bloom and the fragrance of the blossoms filled the air. Cardiff Hill, beyond the village and above it, was green with vegetation, and it lay just far enough away to seem a delectable land, dreamy, reposeful, and inviting.

Tom appeared on the sidewalk with a bucket of whitewash and a long-handled brush. He surveyed the fence. All gladness left him and a deep melancholy settled down upon his spirit. Thirty yards of board fence nine feet high! Life to him seemed hollow, and existence but a burden. Sighing, he dipped his brush and passed it along the topmost plank. He repeated the operation; did it again; compared the insignificant whitewashed streak with the far-reaching continent of unwhitewashed fence, and sat down on a tree-box discouraged.

Jim came skipping out at the gate with a tin pail. He was singing "Buffalo Gals." Bringing water from the town pump had always been hateful work in Tom's eyes before, but now it did not strike him so. He remembered that there was company at the pump. Boys and girls were always there waiting their turns, resting, trading playthings, quarreling, fighting, skylarking. And he remembered that although the pump was only a hundred and fifty yards off, Jim never got back with a bucket of water under an hour — and even then somebody generally had to go after him.

Tom said,

"Say, Jim, I'll fetch the water if you'll do some whitewashing."

Jim shook his head and said,

"Can't Mars' Tom. Ole missis, she tole me I got to go an' git dis water an' not stop foolin' round' wid anybody. She says she spec' Mars' Tom gwine to ax me to whitewash, an' so she tole me go 'long an' 'tend to my own business — she 'lowed *she'd* tend to de whitewashin'."

"Oh, never you mind what she said, Jim. That's the way she always talks. Gimme the bucket — I won't be gone only a minute. *She* won't ever know."

"Oh, I dasn't, Mars' Tom. Ole missis she'd take an' tar de head off'n me. 'Deed she would."

"*She!* She never licks anybody. She whacks 'em over the head with her thimble — but who cares for that, I'd like to know? She talks awful, but talk don't hurt — anyways it don't if she don't cry. Jim, I'll give you a marble. I'll give you a white alley!"

Jim began to waver.

"White alley, Jim! And it's a bully taw."

"My! Dat's a might gay marble, *I* tell you! But Mars' Tom I's powerful 'fraid Ole missis —"

"And besides, if you will, I'll show you my sore toe."

Jim was only human — this attraction was too much for him. He put down his pail, took the white alley, and bent over the toe with absorbing interest while the bandage was being unwound!

In another moment he was flying down the street with his pail and a tingling rear. Tom was whitewashing with vigor, and Aunt Polly was retiring from the field with a slipper in her hand and triumph in her eye.

But Tom's energy did not last. He began to think of the fun he had planned for this day, and his sorrows multiplied. Soon the free boys would come tripping along on all sorts of delicious expeditions, and they would make fun of him for having to work. The very thought of it burnt him like fire. He got out his worldly wealth and examined it — bits of toys, marbles, and trash; enough to buy an exchange of *work*, maybe, but not half enough to buy so much as half an hour of pure freedom. So he returned his meager means to his pocket, and gave up the idea of trying to buy the boys.

At this dark and hopeless moment an inspiration burst upon him! It was nothing less than a great, magnificent inspiration.

Tom took up his brush and went tranquilly to work. Ben Rogers hove in sight presently — the very boy, of all boys, whose ridicule he had been dreading.

Ben was eating an apple, and giving a long, melodious whoop, at intervals, followed by a deep-toned ding-dong-dong, ding-dong-dong, for he was personating a steamboat.

As Ben drew near, he slackened speed.

Tom went on whitewashing and paid no attention to the steamboat.

Ben stared a moment and then said, *"Hi-yi! You're* a stump, ain't you!"

No answer. Tom surveyed his last touch with the eye of an artist; then he gave his brush another gentle sweep and surveyed the result, as before.

Ben ranged up alongside of him.

T.B.

Tom's mouth watered for the apple, but he stuck to his work.

Ben said,

"Hello, old chap, you got to work, hey?"

Tom wheeled suddenly and said, "Why, it's you, Ben! I warn't noticing."

"Say — *I'm* going in a-swimming, I am.
Don't you wish you could? But of course
you'd druther *work* — wouldn't you?
Course you would!"

Tom contemplated the boy a bit, and
said, "What do you call work?"

"Why, ain't *that* work?"

Tom resumed his whitewashing, and
answered carelessly, "Well, maybe it is,
and maybe it ain't. All I know is, it suits
Tom Sawyer.

"Does a boy get a chance to whitewash a fence every day?"

That put the thing in a new light. Ben stopped nibbling his apple.

Tom swept his brush daintily back and forth — stepped back to note the effect — added a touch here and there — criticized the effect again.

Ben was watching every move and getting more and more interested, more and more absorbed.

Presently he said,

"Say, Tom, let *me* whitewash a little."

Tom considered, was about to consent; but he changed his mind.

"Ben, I'd like to, honest injun. Jim wanted to do it, too, but Aunt Polly wouldn't let him.

"You see, Aunt Polly's awful particular about this fence — right here on the street, you know. If it was the back fence I wouldn't mind and *she* wouldn't. Yes, she's awful particular about this fence. It's got to be done very careful. I reckon there ain't one boy in a thousand, maybe two thousand, that can do it the way it's got to be done."

"No — is that so? Oh come, now — lemme just try. Only just a little — I'd let *you*, if you was me, Tom."

"Now don't you see how I'm fixed? If you was to tackle this fence and anything was to happen to it —"

"Oh shucks, I'll be just as careful. Now lemme try. Say — I'll give you the core of my apple."

"Well, here. No, Ben, now don't. I'm afraid —"

"I'll give you *all* of it!"

Tom gave up the brush with reluctance in his face but eagerness in his heart.

And while Ben worked and sweated in
the sun, the retired artist sat on a barrel
in the shade close by, dangled his legs,
munched his apple, and planned the
slaughter of more innocents.

There was no lack of material; boys
happened along every little while. They

came to jeer, but remained to whitewash.
By the time Ben was tired out, Tom had
traded the next chance to Billy Fisher for
a kite, in good repair; and when *he* played
out, Johnny Miller bought in for a dead
rat and a string to swing it with — and so
on, and so on, hour after hour.

And when the middle of the afternoon came, from being a poor, poverty-stricken boy in the morning, Tom was literally rolling in wealth. He had, besides the things before mentioned, twelve marbles, a jew's-harp, a piece of blue bottle glass to look through, a spool cannon, a key that wouldn't unlock anything, a fragment of chalk, a glass stopper of a decanter, a tin soldier, a couple of tadpoles, six firecrackers,

a kitten with only one eye, a brass door-knob, a dog collar — but no dog — the handle of a knife, four pieces of orange-peel, and a dilapidated old window-sash.

He had a nice, good, idle time all the
while — plenty of company — and the
fence had three coats of whitewash on it!
If he hadn't run out of whitewash, he
would have bankrupted every boy in the
village.

Tom said to himself that it was not such a hollow world, after all. He had discovered a great law of human action, without knowing it — namely, that in order to make a man or boy covet a thing, it is only necessary to make the thing difficult to attain. If he had been a great and wise philosopher, like the writer of this story, he would now have comprehended that work consists of whatever a body is *obliged* to do, and that play consists of whatever a body is not obliged to do.